SULKY SUE
by TONY GARTH

Sue was a very sulky little girl. Especially if she didn't get her own way.

If she couldn't have sweets before lunch or the biggest doll in the shop, she sulked.

One day, Sue had a great idea. What she really wanted was a pet dog.

"Mum," she said, "Can I have a dog, please?"

"I'm afraid not, dear," said her Mum.

"It's just not fair," shouted Sue. "You never let me have anything I want."

She sat down in an armchair, with a very loud thump, folded her arms and started to sulk.

Sue sulked until tea time. Then she carried on sulking until it was time for bed. Her Mum and Dad were worried. She'd never sulked for this long before.

Next morning, Sue was still sulking...

"Whatever shall we do?" said Sue's Mum.

"We'd better call the doctor," replied her Dad. "I can't think of anything else."

When the doctor arrived, he examined Sue very, very carefully. He looked in her ears, in her eyes and at her tonsils. He tested her reflexes and made her say "Aahh!"

Then he gave his verdict.

"This is the worst case of the sulks I have ever seen," he said. "The only thing you can do is to make her think of something else."

It was easier said than done.

"I know," said Sue's Dad. "We'll try tickling her. That should do it."

And off he went to find the feather duster.

They tickled and tickled until their arms ached but Sue didn't even smile. She just sat there and sulked.

Next they tried telling funny jokes. But that was no good either. Even the one about the penguin and the two old ladies didn't make Sue laugh. She just sat there and sulked even more.

Her Mum and Dad tried singing and juggling. They even dressed up as magicians and did magic tricks. In fact, they did them rather well. But Sue just sulked and sulked.

They put on an all-singing, all-dancing, musical extravaganza with puppets made from washing-up liquid bottles, sticky tape and string. But it didn't work.

Sulky Sue simply sat and sulked.

They dressed up as clowns and threw buckets of water and custard pies at each other. It was really quite hilarious. But the sulky look on Sue's face didn't change a bit.

Sue's Mum and Dad were exhausted. They'd tried everything they could think of. And none of it made any difference at all.

"It's no use," said Sue's Mum. "I give in. We'll just have to buy her the dog she wants. It's the only thing we can do."

"Leave it to me," replied Sue's Dad. "I know exactly the sort of dog for Sue."

And off he set for the pet shop.

Sue's Mum was right! The minute Sue saw the dear little puppy, she stopped sulking in a flash.

There was just one problem...

The dog her Dad had chosen for her was a very sulky dog indeed!

Look out for the next twelve Little Monsters!

FRIENDLY FRANCO

CLUMSY CLARISSA

BOISTEROUS BILLY

SICKLY SIMON

SERIOUS SADIE

GROW... GAB...

PERFECT PRUDENCE

RUDE ROGER

DANGEROUS DAVE

CURIOUS CALVIN

DIRTY DERMOT

TANT... TABI...